The WISE TOWER Of Bower

by Samantha Cruz

illustrated by
Veen Redwood

© 2021 Samantha Cruz
www.samanthacruzbooks.com

First Edition December 2021
ISBN 9781737722144 (Hardcover)
ISBN 9781737722137 (Paperback)
Valleytap Village Press
Saint Augustine, FL 32080
www.valleytapvillage.com

Don't forget to keep an eye out
for the little yellow birdies!

Tommy was a man as tall as a tree,
but when he was born they didn't know he would be.

As a boy he was average, some were taller than he.
Now, over rows of roofs of houses he could see.

Growing up wasn't easy,
most kids heckled and poked,
and hiding out in his house wasn't fun with his folks.

To play with the kids in the street and tell jokes,
was all that he wanted,
though he'd never dare to provoke.

Tommy grew taller
as he kept getting older.
So tall was he now,
the rooftops at his shoulders.

Everyone poked fun and
with each laugh he grew colder.
He thought to himself,
"One day, I'll make my life up by the boulders"

All of Bower called him crazy,
they all hollered and hooped.
So he'd sit and he'd sit on the steps of his stoop.

He'd look to the sky
at the birds as they'd swoop,
surrounding the trees making one giant loop.

"That's where I belong,
with the birds and the sun."
So up to the boulders they'd see tall Tommy run.

Day after day, with five leaps and a lunge,
he would hop to the top
of the hill called Mount Lund.

The spot that he picked
overlooked the whole town.
The view was so nice he'd thought he'd never go down.

The streets down below
were so busy and loud.
He could never give up what he'd build in the clouds.

It was a house made for trees.
The townsfolk called it The Great Tower.
Tall Tommy was a tree
from the town they called Bower.

And although growing up
they all made him feel sour,
he knew nevermore could he give them that power.

He now had a job to be happy and free,
to look out for all others
who were taller than trees.

And to his surprise there were others he'd see,
heads rising above,
some even taller than he.

He knew he wasn't alone as tall kids came to talk.
They had the same troubles
with mean kids on the block.

Tommy told them his story as he took them on walks,
and he taught them to never to give up
no matter how hard they all balk.

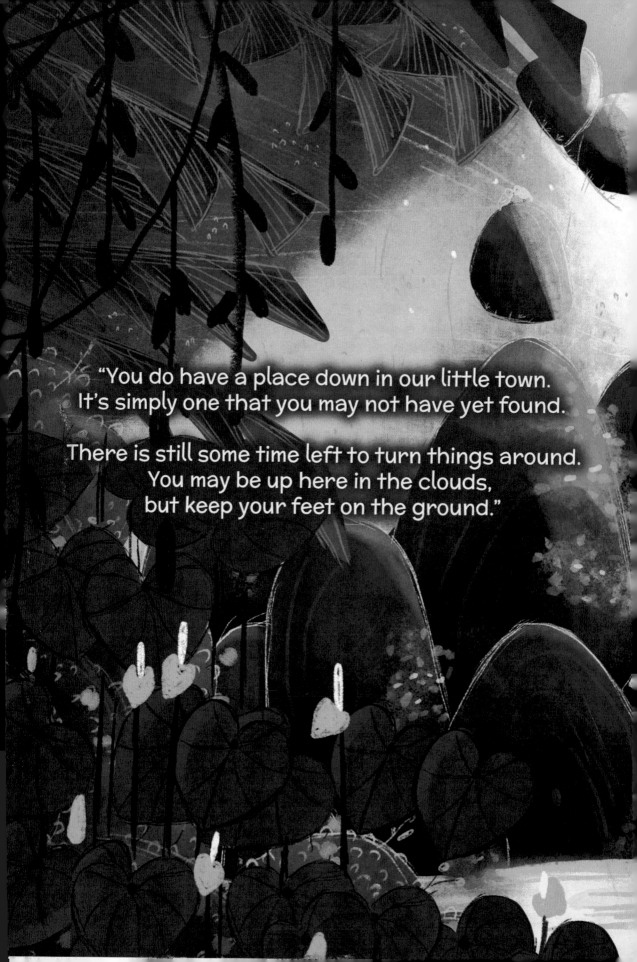

"You do have a place down in our little town.
It's simply one that you may not have yet found.

There is still some time left to turn things around.
You may be up here in the clouds,
but keep your feet on the ground."

Tommy thought to himself
"I can help these kids make it,
even if, growing up, I myself could not face it."

So day after day
the tall kids came to sit,
and day after day Tommy told them never to quit.

Tommy's wise words rang true
as he watched the kids play.
He'd sit and he'd wonder if he'd go back there one day.

But as he thought a bit more,
he realized he found his own way.
Tommy, the wise tree in the Tower of Bower, he'd stay.

THE WISE TOWER OF BOWER

Tommy and the Townsfolk

There is a BIG difference between Tommy and the Townsfolk. Yup, you guessed it. Tommy is very tall compared to everyone else and the people of the town don't like him because of it. It seems silly, right? Why would anyone want to be so mean to a nice boy like Tommy? The reason can be as simple as looking different than everyone else, but there can also be many other reasons why this happens.

In the town of Bower, the townsfolk make poor choices in how they treat Tommy, choices that leave him feeling isolated and alone. What the townsfolk do to Tommy is called social bullying.

Although there are different types of bullying, social bullying is when an individual or a group:
- leaves someone out on purpose
- tells others not to be friends with the person they target
- points fingers or spreads rumors about the person they target
- embarrasses their target in public

Other types of bullying include physical bullying (hurting someone's body or their things) and verbal bullying (writing or saying mean things about another).

Luckily, we can all help!

Did you know that we can all help to prevent bullying behavior?
Let's take a quick look at the 3Cs:

Communication
You can chat directly with an adult about bullying! Sometimes all it takes is a quick 15 minute chat with an adult to help assure you that when a problem arises, you aren't alone. Here are some questions to get you started:
- What was one good thing that happened today? Any bad things?
- What are you good at? What would do you like best about yourself?
- What does "bullying" mean to you?
- Describe what kids who bully are like. Why do you think people bully?
- What do you usually do when you see bullying going on?
- Do you ever see kids at your school being bullied by other kids? How does it make you feel?

Companionship
We all need companionship! Take time to explore the activities that you love to participate in. Talk to an adult about what interests you and together you may find ways to meet up with other kids who have similar interests. The more confidence we build through friendships, the more we can help protect ourselves from bullying.

Courtesy
Courtesy is more than just being polite! We learn acceptable behaviors from the adults around us, so choose positive role models that show respect for themselves and kindness, tolerance, and forgiveness of others, too. These positive role models can be parents, other members of your family, teachers, coaches, and more. Learn how to be courteous from these positive role models. If you are unsure of who to turn to, simply ask a parent or a teacher! You can also show courtesy towards others by being a helper when you see others in need and using simple manners, like saying please and thank you every chance you get!

For more information, visit **www.stopbullying.gov**

ABOUT THE AUTHOR

Samantha Cruz, born January 23, 1991, grew up in Bunnell, Florida on her father's farm. She is the third born of four girls, who still live in and around the area. As children growing up on the family farm, a lack of neighbors led to endless imaginative adventures amongst the siblings, from building forts in the woods, to creating "cousins' plays" for the extended family to enjoy.

Samantha's first book (about an alien she found behind a dumpster) was published through a student publishing project in the second grade and although her spark for writing didn't reveal itself until her early 20s, her imagination, creative nature, and silly tendencies never dwindled. Soon she would find herself in pursuit of a teaching career, with her first assignment in a second grade classroom.

For the next 6 years she continued her career as an educator, with her primary assignments in middle school science and elementary language arts. The closer she became with early school aged children, learning of their aspirations, their own perceived roadblocks to success, as well as their social tendencies, the more inspiration she garnered for her books. During this time, she learned not only about the interests of her students, but also gained first hand knowledge of the pervasive fixed mindset that plagues much of our youth today.

Her first book, Fin the Fern (2018), follows the early growth of a fern who, with the help of a benevolent dove, is encouraged through her first moments in a new and vibrant world. Fin the Fern carries such themes as kindness, mentorship, and love while other themes throughout her works include exploration and imagination. Perhaps born out of her experiences as a teacher and her own scientific interests, her children's stories often fall on the spectrum between literature and science, with the most recent series, Addison Rue and the Big Dreaming Book, taking young readers on an adventure of discovery in the fields of Science, Technology, Engineering, Art, and Math (STEAM).

Samantha lives in Saint Augustine, FL with her husband, Chris, and two energetic pups, Roxy and Bailey. With her husband's unwavering support, Samantha now pursues writing full-time.

SAMANTHA CRUZ

Author

Made in the USA
Las Vegas, NV
08 February 2022

43495382R00019